The Cake Case

HAILEY SCRAGG • LISA PERRETT

Kate made a cape.

The cake is not on the dish!

Kate will take the case.

A path!

Kate will chase
the cake.

Ace! Zane!

What is on
your faces?

Zane and Ace ate
the cake!

Kate and Dad will bake a new cake.

Now cake is on
Kate's face!

Ace	cape	Kate('s)
ate	case	made
bake	chase	take
cake	face(s)	Zane

| Dad | not | will |
| dish | on | |

a	new	the
and	now	what
is	path	your